1

John Bolting looked into the mirror for the tenth time. 'Cathy, will you marry me?' he said. No. That was no good. He couldn't ask her just like that.

How did you ask someone to marry you? At the pictures it all looked so easy. The moon would be shining. The woman would be gazing into the man's eyes and somehow everything would come out right. But it wasn't like that in real life.

John peered into the mirror again and tried to smooth down his mop of curly hair. What a clot he was. After all, he told Cathy he loved her nearly every time they met. He did not need to stand in front of a mirror to find words for that. So why was this so hard?

He turned to the mirror again for one last try. 'Cathy,' he said. 'Would you become Cathy Bolting?' Ah, now that sounded nice. Yes. He would ask her that way.

He laughed to himself. Thank goodness Cathy couldn't see him doing all this. She would think he had gone mad. Never mind. He had found the right words.

Now all he had to do was say them. Cathy Bolting. It sounded good. He said the name to himself over and over again. If she would marry him, he would be the happiest man alive.

He looked at his watch. It was time to go. They had planned to meet in the park at seven. Quickly he pulled on his coat and ran downstairs. 'I'm off, mum. Bye.' Mrs Bolting came into the hall. 'John, I thought you had gone ages ago,' she said. 'You're late, aren't you? Don't you usually meet Cathy at seven?' John stared at her. 'Yes, but it's only ten to seven now.' Mrs Bolting shook her head. 'It's ten to eight, dear,' she said. 'Your watch must have stopped.'

In the park, Cathy Walker had moved from her place by the tree. She was sitting on the bench now, looking all around for John. But there was no one to be seen.

Cathy could feel a lump coming into her throat. She had been here an hour now. What could have happened to make John so late? In all the ten months they had been going out together, he had never been late. Not like this. Perhaps he wasn't coming, or perhaps something awful had happened to him.

Suddenly she heard the sound of running. Someone was coming up behind her. She turned round and there was John. 'Oh Cathy, I'm sorry I'm so late,' he said. 'My watch had stopped.'

He sat down beside her, puffing for breath. It was then that he saw tears running down her cheeks. 'Cathy Bolting,' he said. 'You're crying. What ever is the matter?' She put her arms around him, and then stopped. 'John,' she said suddenly. 'What did you just call me?'

'Cathy Bolting,' he said. Then he stopped too. 'Oh Cathy, what a mess I've made of everything. I've spent the last hour trying to work out how to ask you to marry me. Then I go and do a thing like that. I've messed it all up.'

Cathy smiled and shook her head. 'You haven't messed it up at all,' she whispered. 'I think it's a lovely way to be asked.' She looked at him. 'Don't you want to know the answer?' she said, giving him a small punch in the ribs. John nodded. 'Yes,' she grinned. 'Yes please.'

2

John looked up at the sky. It was a bright morning and the sun was shining. As they walked to the bus stop, hand in hand, he felt very happy. They were going to buy a ring, an engagement ring. 'Are you happy, Cathy?' he said. She nodded and smiled. It was just what they both wanted.

The first shop they went into was the largest in town. The woman at the counter smiled at them kindly. 'Good morning, can I help you?' 'Well, I hope you can,' said John, grinning. 'We would like to buy a ring.' 'Well, all our stock is in the window,' said the woman. 'Still, if you tell me what you want, I will go and look for you.' She could see these two would need a lot of help.

'Well,' said John. 'We would like an engagement ring, please. One with a blue stone, I think.' He turned to Cathy. 'That's right, isn't it?' She smiled and nodded. 'I'll just go and see what we have,' said the woman.

'Is that OK?' John said when she had gone. 'Yes, but don't spend too much money on it,' said Cathy. 'Not just for a ring. We have to buy the flat yet!'

Just then the woman came back. She had a whole tray of rings. They looked at them carefully. Cathy didn't know which one she wanted. Suddenly John spotted a ring on the end of the tray. 'Try this one on, Cathy. This is lovely.' Cathy picked it up. It was a beautiful blue. But it didn't fit. 'I'm afraid I can't get that one in a bigger size,' said the woman. 'It's the only one I have.'

They left the shop. It was sad, but there were lots of other places to go. They spent most of the day looking for rings. In the end they were tired out. All they wanted was to sit down. 'Come on. Let's get something to eat,' John said, putting his arm round Cathy.

They were just going into the main street when they passed a shop they had not seen before. It was not a new shop. It was a second-hand shop. It had all sorts of things in the window. Old carved tables. Beautiful mirrors. Dusty old books. But the thing that caught Cathy's eye was a ring. A beautiful ring, lying on soft velvet. She stopped and stared at it. There was a shine in the dark stone. She could not take her eyes away from it. She had seen a lot of rings that day. Beautiful rings. But this was the first one she had really wanted. 'John,' she whispered. 'Just look at that.'

3

They gazed at the ring together. 'It's very beautiful,' John agreed. 'But it's second-hand. Don't you want a new one?' 'Oh no,' said Cathy. Her eyes were shining. 'It doesn't matter if it's not new. It's the best one we've seen.' 'Well we must not get too excited,' John said. 'It may not be the right size.'

She led him into the shop. It smelt old, as if it had not been dusted for years. The sun was still shining outside. But inside it was dark. There did not seem to be anyone about. Cathy looked round for a bell. But there was not one on the counter. She opened the door and then shut it again with a bang. But still no one came.

'Well, perhaps we could look at the ring while we wait,' Cathy whispered. John smiled. He could see she wanted the ring. She climbed over the small tables and finally got to the window. There it was, lying on the velvet. The stone was so dark it looked black. She made her way back to John, and gave him the ring. He took her hand.

'Shut your eyes,' he said. Slowly and carefully, he slipped the ring on her finger. Her wedding finger.

Cathy could feel the ring, cold and strange, as it went on. For a moment she felt weak. As if she had to sit down. She could not think where she was or what she was doing. Then she opened her eyes and saw the ring. There it was on her finger. As if, in some way, it had been there always. She looked at the large black stone. In the middle, there was a shine, a glow. It drew her towards it. It seemed to belong to her already.

'It's no good, Cathy. This one's too big.' Her thoughts were stopped by John. His voice seemed far away. With an effort she tried to think, to bring her mind back to the shop and him. 'It's not too big,' she said at last. 'It's just that my hands are cold, that's all.' 'Oh Cathy!' John did not know what to say. He could see the ring was too big but he could also see how much she wanted it.

At that moment there was a sound in the shop. It came from a corner. John peered into the darkness. He could just make out the shape of a chair. He peered again. There was a man in the chair. Had he been in the shop all the time? How odd. John made his way across to the corner. Now he could see it was a rocking chair that had made the sound. And there, in the chair, was an old, old man. He was rocking to and fro, just smiling in the darkness.

4

'Have you been there all the time?' said John crossly. 'Didn't you hear us bang the door?' The old man said nothing. He just looked at John. His eyes were sad and distant. Then slowly he nodded his head. John could see the long deep lines on his face. He looked as old as the things in the shop.

John shuddered. He did not like the look of the old man. There was something about him. The way he smiled. The way he looked.

The old man turned towards Cathy. 'I see the lady likes my ring,' he said, and smiled. John looked at Cathy. She was at the other side of the shop, just standing there looking at the ring. Hadn't she seen him go to the corner? Couldn't she hear him talking to the old man? It wasn't like Cathy.

The old man smiled. 'She only has eyes for the ring,' he said. 'You must get it for her. Now she has seen it, she must have it. Now it is on her finger, she must keep it.' The old man was not smiling now. His eyes were distant again, his mouth set. John could feel himself getting angry. 'You have been here all the time,' he said. 'You know

it doesn't fit. It's too big.' The old man shook his
head. Slowly he got out of the chair. 'Come with
me,' he said, 'I will show you.'

Cathy was still looking at the ring, lost in a world of
her own. She had not heard John talking. She
looked up in surprise when she saw the old man, and
for a moment her mind was taken off the ring. She
stared at the man. He was old. And yet there was
something about his eyes which held her, which for a
moment made her catch her breath. His eyes were
so soft and sad. They seemed to be telling her
something. And as she looked at him she could see
that once he had been young and handsome. She
smiled at him, almost shyly. He smiled back.

'I see you like my ring,' he said. 'Let me have a
look, will you?' Very gently he took her hand.
John watched. The man looked at the ring carefully
and then at Cathy. 'It is perfect,' he said, turning
to John. 'It fits the lady as if it were made for
her.' John stared down at Cathy's hand. He felt the
ring and her cold finger. The ring did seem to fit.
But how could it? A few moments ago it had been
too big.

John didn't like what was happening. There was
something very odd about it all. He turned to Cathy

but she did not see him. She was looking at the ring. She could not seem to take her eyes away from it. 'It looks as if your young lady must have my ring,' said the old man. 'A lot of people have wanted it, but I would not sell it to them. Your lady is different,' he said, turning to look at Cathy. 'You may have it for ten pounds.'

John didn't know what to do. He knew how much Cathy wanted the ring, but something made him feel cold inside. Perhaps it was the old man. Perhaps it was the ring. Suddenly he could stand it no longer. He had to get out of the shop. He had to get Cathy away.

He grabbed her hand and took off the ring. He almost threw it on the counter. He didn't look at the old man. Cathy did not know what was happening. Before she could stop him, she felt John half pushing her, half pulling her, out of the shop.

Alone in his chair, the old man rocked to and fro. His eyes were far away, distant. He was remembering a time long ago. A time of great love and happiness with his young love, Lorna. He could see her in his mind. Her soft brown hair high on her head, her grey eyes looking only at him. She was gone now. Dead. But how like her the girl in the shop had been.

5

The light outside almost hit them. It had been so dark in the shop. Cathy still did not know why all this was happening. She could feel John pulling her up the street, but why? 'John, what's the matter with you?' She looked into his eyes. She was puzzled.

'I don't want you to have the ring, Cathy, and that's that,' he said finally. 'I'm sorry. I know you liked it. And I love you and want you to have what you want. But not that ring. That's all.' His eyes were kind but firm. Cathy was wide awake now but she still could not understand him. She shook her head. 'Why?' she asked. 'I don't understand you.'

John was silent for a time. 'Look, Cathy,' he said in the end. 'I don't know why. I didn't like the old man, perhaps that's it. Or the way the ring seemed to get smaller. I didn't like the whole set-up.' He stopped. 'I didn't like the way the old man said it was just right for you, either,' he added. 'It was a beautiful ring and ten pounds was too little for it.' He looked at Cathy. Her face was so sad and puzzled.

'Come on, Cathy,' he said, and hugged her, and tried to grin. 'Come and have something to eat. I'll get

13

you the biggest plate of egg and chips they have in the shop. Just for you.'

But Cathy did not move. 'Stop it,' she said. 'The old man was kind. He could see I liked the ring. He wanted me to have it. That is why he was going to let us buy it for ten pounds. Anyway, old rings don't cost as much as new ones. As for the ring being too big and then just right, what are you talking about, John Bolting? Have you gone mad? My hand was cold at first. That's all.'

He looked at her. He didn't know what to do, or what to say. He loved her. 'Oh Cathy,' he whispered, and put his arms round her. But she threw them off. 'Go away,' she said, full of anger. 'You can't love me. Go away.' She turned her back on him and started to run down the street.

6

When Cathy got home she was tired out. Her eyes were red with crying and she didn't want to see anyone. She tried to slip upstairs without being seen, but her mother heard the door. 'Is that you, Cathy?' Mrs Walker came into the hall. Then she saw Cathy's eyes. 'Why, whatever is the matter, dear? Has anything happened?'

How silly, thought Cathy. She can see something's happened. She sniffed. 'No, it's all right, mum,' she said out loud. 'I'm just a bit tired, that's all. I'll go to bed now.' She tried to sound bright. But she didn't feel like talking.

'Can I bring you a cup of tea, dear?' said Mrs Walker. 'No thanks, mum.' Tea, always tea, at any time of the day! Cathy was at the top of the stairs now. 'Good-night.' It was all she could do to stop herself from sobbing. She undressed and flung herself on to her bed. She was so tired and unhappy.

Mrs Walker went back to her book. But all she could think about was Cathy. Was John messing her about? She didn't want Cathy to get hurt. Mrs Walker knew what that was like, only too well.

That night was a bad one for Cathy. She tossed and turned and cried. Sometimes she could see the ring in her mind. And sometimes John, looking at her with sad eyes. Then she would turn again and sob. He couldn't love her, that was it. And she so wanted the ring. If he loved her he would buy it. She couldn't bear it. She wished she could sleep. But everything went round and round in her mind. Over and over again. All night. At last, just before morning, she fell asleep.

Mrs Walker had a bad night, too. She kept dreaming about her own past. The next morning she came down to the kitchen. The yellow sun streamed in through the window and hurt her eyes. She was tired. She needed a cup of tea. She went to the doorstep to see if the milk had come. Sometimes the milkman was late on a Sunday.

The milk had come, but there was something else on the doorstep, too. It was a little box in brown paper. It must have come by hand. She looked at the name on it. 'Miss Cathy Walker,' it said. Mrs Walker was pleased. Perhaps it would cheer Cathy up.

'Cathy!' Mrs Walker ran upstairs, with the small box in her hand. 'Cathy, dear, there's something for you,' she said, and went into the room.

Cathy sat up. Her face was white and her eyes red. She could not think. She wasn't quite awake. Then slowly she remembered John and the ring, and felt sick.

Then she saw the box. Her mother had put it on the bed. Cathy looked at it hard, and then her heart jumped. Quickly she started to open it. She threw the brown paper on to the floor. Yes, there, underneath the paper, was a small black box. She held her breath. Inside was the ring. Her ring, shining darkly in the light of the bedroom. Mrs Walker had a good look. So John had made up his mind at last! Cathy flung her arms round her mother. 'Oh mum,' she said, hugging her. 'He loves me. He loves me.'

7

One moment Cathy looked sad, the next moment she was laughing. Mrs Walker didn't know what to make of it. Still, it didn't matter now. She was just pleased to see Cathy was happy. Perhaps now everything would be all right.

'Are you going to tell me what it's all about?' she said, sitting down on the bed. But Cathy did not hear. Her eyes were on the ring. Mrs Walker got up and crept out of the room. Perhaps Cathy would like to be alone now. She shut the door quietly.

Cathy did not hear her mother go. She just picked up the ring and slipped it on to her finger. For a moment, she felt strange and weak. But she had the ring and that was all that seemed to matter. She smiled and gazed at the stone. Her eyes were drawn deep into its glow.

Time passed as she lay there. Slowly, very slowly, thoughts of John and her mother and her home seemed to fade. She could hear her mother downstairs. But in some way, the noise seemed no longer part of her life.

The world began to spin around her. Pictures passed through her mind, blurs at first, shapes she did not know. They rose and fell in front of her eyes and she longed for them to stay still, just for a moment, so she could make them out.

Then, at last, they began to slow down and before her eyes she began to see all sorts of strange things and places she had never known. There was a beautiful garden with a summer house, and a tree with a swing hanging down from its branches. Even the light was soft and green. She could almost smell the sweet scent of the flowers and hear the birds singing.

Cathy felt very warm and happy. She clapped her hands. In some strange way she felt she knew that swing. And yet she had never seen it before.

She jumped out of bed. Her eyes were laughing and her heart singing. She almost danced to her dressing table. Then she sat down on the stool in front of her mirror. Picking up her brush, she swept her soft brown hair high on to her head. She did it quickly, almost without thinking, as if she had done it for years. Then she looked into the mirror. Her grey eyes were lost in thought.

8

Downstairs, Mrs Walker was thinking back to when she had first had her own ring. Funny old life! You never could tell what might happen.

She looked up to see John coming to the door. He did not look very happy. So what was happening with this ring? 'Can I see Cathy?' he said. 'Yes, of course, dear,' said Mrs Walker. 'Come in. She's still in bed, I'm afraid. But do go up.'

John went upstairs slowly. What mood would Cathy be in? He was frightened she would not see him again, after last night.

He tapped on the bedroom door. 'Are you there, Cathy?' he said, in a whisper. But there was no answer. Perhaps she was still asleep. He would creep in quietly, and give her a surprise.

But when he opened the door, it was John who was surprised. Cathy was sitting at the dressing table. But it hardly looked like the Cathy he knew. She was wearing a long pink night-dress. Her hair was high on her head and her eyes seemed dazed and distant.

She did not seem to hear him. When he touched her back and looked into her eyes, she did not move or seem to see him. He could not believe it. 'Cathy,' he said. 'Cathy!' and he shook her.

Slowly she seemed to wake up. She looked at him, dazed. 'Cathy,' he said again. 'What is the matter? Why are you like this? Are you still angry with me?' He looked at her, longing for a smile or a word.

Slowly, very slowly, as if out of a dream, Cathy felt herself drawn back to her home and her room. She could hear John's voice, worried and urgent. And now she could see John's face, and his eyes searching hers.

'Oh John,' she whispered, 'I think I've been dreaming.' Now she could remember everything. How much she loved him. The row last night and the ring this morning. 'Oh John. I don't know what has been happening,' she whispered. 'I had an awful night last night and now I don't feel very well. I'm sorry for the things I said yesterday.' She put her arms round him and cried softly on his shoulder.

For a moment John could say nothing. But he could feel his heart lift with happiness. She loved him. That was all he wanted to hear. He held her tightly.

Then Cathy looked up. 'John. There s something else I haven't said,' she whispered. 'Thank you for getting the ring. I didn't deserve it, after everything I said.'

John looked puzzled. 'The ring?' he said. 'What do you mean?' She smiled. 'Thank you for the ring,' she said and gave him a hug. 'It's so beautiful.' She held her hand out for him to see. 'When it came this morning, I knew you loved me.'

John stared down, shocked and puzzled. He took her hand and looked at the ring carefully and then at her. 'Cathy,' he said. 'I don't understand. Where did you get the ring?'

Cathy sat up. 'John,' she said. 'I know you're teasing me but I don't feel very well. You got the ring. You know you did.'

John stared down at her hand and then at her. He was silent for a moment. 'Cathy,' he said finally, 'I didn't buy the ring.'

9

They sat there for a moment, too stunned to talk. Trying to think. Trying to work things out. If John had not got the ring, who had?

John had an idea. 'Did you tell anyone about it?' he said. 'Did you tell your mum, or anyone when you got home? Or on the bus? Or when you left me?' Cathy shook her head. 'Think carefully, Cathy. Are you sure?' But Cathy was sure. She had been too upset to talk.

John could see that Cathy was looking pale and tired. 'Listen,' he said kindly, 'someone must have got it for us as a present, but I want to find out who it was. Until I know, would you do something for me?'

He picked up her hand and held it in his. 'Will you take the ring off? Just until we know who got it. I won't take it away. I want you to have it. I just don't want you to wear it until we know who got it.'

Cathy nodded. She was tired now, almost too tired to think or care. She just wanted to sleep. So John helped her to get into bed. Then he took her hand. He would take the ring off, himself.

But it would not come. It was too tight. He pulled, but it hardly moved. 'Oh I'll do it myself,' said Cathy. He was hurting her and she felt cross with him. But she could not get it off. She peered at it closely. It had been easy to put on, but she could not get it off. She sank back into the bed. 'I'm tired, John. I'm hot and tired. I'll take the ring off later. I'm sorry. I had a bad night, and now I want some sleep.' She shut her eyes. It was all she could do to keep awake.

John bit his lips. Perhaps he was being silly, but he wanted that ring off. He went to the bathroom to get some soap. That would do the trick.

But it didn't work. John sat there trying. Soap and water was dripping on to the bed and Cathy was half asleep. He now hated the feel of the ring. The dark stone glinted up at him. The ring seemed to be getting tighter, not looser.

He stood up. Perhaps he was making a fuss. He didn't care. He knew what he was going to do. He bent down and kissed Cathy on the cheek. 'Don't worry,' he said. 'You go to sleep now. I will come back this evening. I love you, Cathy.' Quietly he closed the door.

But Cathy heard nothing. She had sunk into a deep sleep. A dark sleep. Through the darkness of her dreams she could see a glint of light far away. And in that light, there was a shape. She could feel herself pulled towards it. Nearer and nearer. It was a strange feeling, and the nearer she got to the light, the further away everything seemed. Her room, her home, everything she knew seemed to slip away as she was drawn towards the light.

10

John did not stop to talk to Mrs Walker. He knew just what he had to do. He was going to that shop. It was Sunday, he knew that, but sometimes that sort of shop was open at odd times. He had to see that man. He had to know who had sent the ring.

When he reached the shop, it was shut. He peered in at the window, and banged on the door. He could hear footsteps coming. Slowly the door was unlocked, and a girl looked out. She looked puzzled. 'We're not open on Sundays,' she said. 'There's just something I want to ask about, that's all,' said John.

The girl could see he was worried. 'How can I help you?' she said. Quickly John looked around. 'Well, it's really the old man I want to see. Is he here?' 'Old man?' said the girl. 'Who do you mean?'

John told her about Saturday. He did not tell her everything, just the main facts. She looked puzzled. 'What time did all this happen?' she said. 'About 4 o'clock,' he said. The girl shook her head. 'Oh no, it can't have been. We shut at one.'

John was stunned. He peered into the corner. 'Did
you have a rocking chair for sale, over there?' he
said. The girl shook her head. 'No. I think you
must have been to another shop.'

He knew the girl was trying to help. He turned to
go. 'Just one thing,' he said. 'Did you have a ring
for sale?' 'No. We don't often have rings,' the girl
said. 'We haven't had one for a long time.'

There was only one thing in John's head now. He
had to get back to Cathy, quickly. There was
something very strange about that ring. They must
get it off Cathy's finger as soon as they could. He
couldn't even wait for the bus. He would run all
the way back to Cathy's house.

Mrs Walker heard the bell ring. John didn't wait to
tell her anything. He just rushed upstairs. 'I have to
see Cathy,' he called back. Cathy's face was pale
and lost in sleep. Gently, John picked up her hand.
The ring was so tight it was digging into her skin.
'Cathy,' he said. 'Cathy, wake up.'

Far, far away, Cathy could hear a voice. She seemed
to know it . . . and yet she could not remember.
All she could see in her mind was a light. It drew

her towards it. 'Forget everything and come to me,' it seemed to say. She stared in her dream. There seemed to be something there. Was it a chair? She stared again. A chair, coming nearer. A chair that seemed to move to and fro in the light.

11

John had to act fast. That ring had to come off.
He ran downstairs. 'Mrs Walker, have you got
something for cutting metal? Anything. Quick.'
She couldn't think what he was asking for. She just
pointed to her drawer of tools. 'All the things are
in there, dear. But what do you want it for?' 'I
can't stop now,' said John. 'Just help me to find
something. Quickly.'

He was pulling everything out of the drawer, all over
the kitchen floor. He saw what he wanted and
grabbed it. Mrs Walker was left standing in the
kitchen, not knowing what was going on.

For half an hour John worked on the ring, trying to
grip it, trying to cut it. Cathy seemed lost in sleep.
A sleep so deep that she couldn't even feel John's
hands, gripping hers.

Finally John gave up. There was no way he could
cut the ring off Cathy's finger. He looked at her
sleeping. It was not normal to sleep like that. He
put his face close to hers. She was breathing, but
only just. In that moment, he knew she was dying.
He knew that, in some way, the ring was killing her.

Fear gripped at his heart. He had to do something.
He loved her. He could not live without her. A
new fear took over. There was only one thing left
for him to do. He felt sick inside. But he knew it
was the only hope. Slowly he left the room. He
was going downstairs for a knife. A very sharp knife.

Cathy was a long way away now. The glow of light
was getting brighter all the time, shining on the
rocking chair. She felt warm inside as it came nearer.
She could make out someone sitting in the chair.
Someone that she liked. Someone she wanted to see.
Someone who liked her and wanted her to have what
she wanted.

She smiled as he came closer. It was the old man.
The old man from the shop. Yet as she looked at
him, he seemed to change. He was no longer an old
man, but young and handsome. His soft eyes did
not look sad any more, but were smiling at her.
'Come to me,' he said. 'Come to me, Lorna. All
this is your home now. The garden, the swing, the
summer-house. I have been waiting for you such a
long time. I love you, Lorna.' He held out his
arms to her.

'I'm coming,' said Cathy. 'I want to come back to
you.' Her eyes were fixed on the young man, on

his soft eyes and gentle smile. She held out her arms to him. She wanted to touch him. She wanted to be in his arms.

John ran up the stairs, a knife in his hands. His teeth were gritted. He had made up his mind, and he was going to do it. He ran into the room. Cathy was still on the bed, but her eyes were open and there was a smile on her face. For a moment John felt there might be hope. But not for long. Cathy seemed to be staring at something far away. She lifted out her arms. John could see the ring on her finger. It was shining brightly now, as if there was a light coming out of it.

Quickly he put a book on the bed, a hard, strong book. Then, carefully, he stretched her finger on to it. All the time the stone glinted up at him, shining into his eyes. With both hands, he lifted the knife into the air and then stopped. Could he really cut off her finger? Could he do this to Cathy? Feeling sick inside, he shut his eyes for a moment. Perhaps there was nothing the matter with the ring. Perhaps he was going mad.

In that short time, Cathy seemed to have changed. Now her face was white and her open eyes seemed fixed, like glass. The ring on her finger was like a

ball of fire. John let out a cry of fear. 'Cathy!'
he screamed at the top of his voice. 'Cathy!'

Without thinking any more, John gripped the knife
in his hands. Then with all his strength he brought
it down on to her finger. Three times he had to
raise the knife above his head, and three times bring
it down.

Then it was done. The finger dropped on to the
floor with a soft thud. Blood gushed from the hand.

John fell to the floor. All his strength had gone.
He lay there, looking at the small white finger, and
sobbed. He did not look at Cathy. There was no
need to. He knew he was too late. She was dead.

CLASSIC **Spirals**

The **Ring**

Susan Duberley

First edition published in 1981 by:
Hutchinson Education

Reprinted in 1991 by:
Stanley Thornes (Publishers) Ltd
ISBN 0 7487 1003 5

Second edition published in 2001 by:
Nelson Thornes Ltd
Delta Place
27 Bath Road
CHELTENHAM
GL53 7TH
United Kingdom

01 02 03 04 05 / 10 9 8 7 6 5 4 3 2 1

A catalogue record for this book is available from the British Library

ISBN 0 7487 6427 5

Printed and bound in Great Britain by Martins the Printers